For Leann and Brian
R.P.M.

For Enid and for Wilf
C.B.

First published in the United States 1993
by Dial Books for Young Readers
A Division of Penguin Books USA Inc.
375 Hudson Street
New York, New York 10014

Published in Great Britain by Victor Gollancz Ltd
Text copyright © 1993 by Rita Phillips Mitchell
Pictures copyright © 1993 by Caroline Binch
All rights reserved
Printed in Hong Kong
1 3 5 7 9 10 8 6 4 2

Library of Congress Cataloging in Publication Data
Mitchell, Rita Phillips.
Hue Boy / story by Rita Phillips Mitchell ;
pictures by Caroline Binch.
p.   cm.
Summary: Everyone in little Hue Boy's
island village has suggestions on how to help him grow,
but he learns to stand tall in a way all his own.
ISBN 0-8037-1448-3
[1. Size—Fiction. 2. Growth—Fiction. 3. Islands—Fiction.]
I. Binch, Caroline, ill. II. Title.
PZ7.M6948Hu 1993 [E]—dc20 92-18560 CIP AC

HUE BOY

Rita Phillips Mitchell

pictures by

Caroline Binch

Dial Books for Young Readers New York

Little Hue Boy was big news in his village. He was so small that all his friends towered over him. Every morning Hue Boy's mama measured him.

"Come, I must measure you before you go to school," she said. "Stand straight against the wall."

It did not matter how straight Hue Boy stood, he remained the same size—very small. He didn't grow at all, at all.

"Oh lawd!" cried Hue Boy's mama. "I wish your papa was home. He would know what to do about this."

But Hue Boy knew his papa was working on a ship, far away.

Then one day Mama said, "Hue Boy, if you want to grow tall, you must eat fresh vegetables and fruit every day."

"Like pumpkins?" said Hue Boy. "I like pumpkin soup."

"Pumpkins are good. But what about spinach, Hue Boy?"

"Yuck!" Hue Boy said. "I don't like spinach, Mama! I'd rather have fruit, like mangoes and melons."

"And pineapples and sapodillas, I suppose?" said his mama.

"Mm, yum, yum," said Hue Boy.

"How about sweetsops, cashews, and craboos?" his mama asked.

"Yes!" said Hue Boy. "And don't forget guavas or tamarinds, either."

"I won't, Hue Boy," said Mama.

Hue Boy was soon eating everything his mama gave him. Pumpkin soup was delicious, but he enjoyed eating fruit best.

Still, Hue Boy didn't grow one little bit. He didn't grow at all, at all.

On Hue Boy's birthday Gran gave him a special present.
  "I've made you new clothes," she said. "You'll soon grow
into them."
  Hue Boy tried on the clothes. They felt a little loose.
  "Lawdy! You look taller already," said Gran.

Then one morning their neighbor Carlos said, "I know, Hue Boy. Some stretching exercises will do the trick. Ten minutes a day. That's all you need to do."

And so Hue Boy began to do all sorts of exercises. He stretched as much as he could.

Still, Hue Boy didn't grow one little bit. He didn't grow at all, at all.

At school his classmates chanted:
        "Heels, heels, high-heeled shoes,
            Needed for the smallest boy in school."
Hue Boy looked down. But Miss Harper the teacher said,

"Stuff and nonsense! Just ignore them, Hue Boy. You'll be growing soon enough."

Still, Hue Boy didn't grow one little bit. He didn't grow at all, at all.

Mama was worried. "I don't like you being teased, Hue Boy," she said. "Come, we must look for some help."

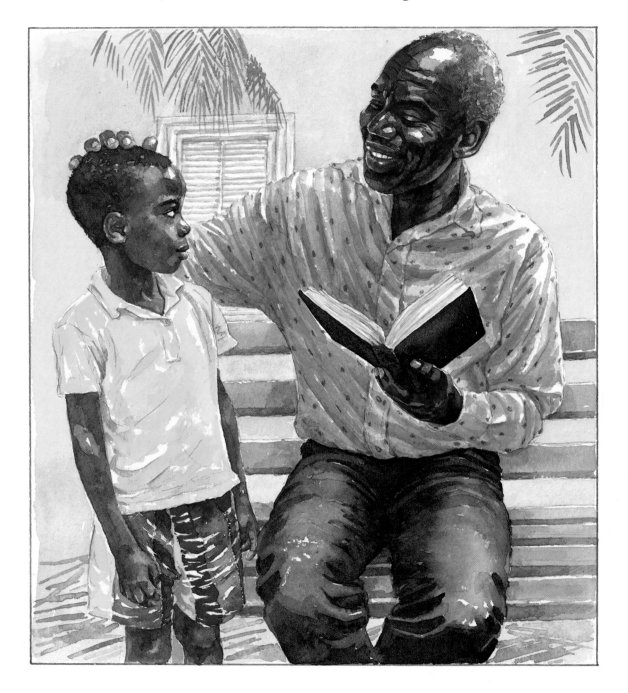

First they went to see the wisest man in the village. "Please," said Mama, "can you help Hue Boy to grow like other children?"

The wise man looked at Hue Boy from head to toe. Then from toe to head. "Well, Hue Boy," he said. "Where help is not needed, no help can be given."

Next they visited Doctor Gamas. He examined Hue Boy thoroughly. Then he said, "There is absolutely nothing wrong with you, Hue Boy. Some people are short and perfectly healthy, you know."

"Lawdy," cried Mama. "This problem seems to be bigger than this village!" She thought carefully. "We ought to try Miss Frangipani the healer," she said. "Maybe she can help."
Hue Boy sighed. "I hope so."

"Miss Frangipani," said Mama.
"Please! Can you do something for
Hue Boy to make him grow?"

"No problem," said Miss Frangipani.
"I alone hold the secret to growing!"

Miss Frangipani placed a hand on
Hue Boy's head and said:

"Ooooo! Ooooo!
Grow-o, Grow-o.
A touch of the hand,
A wish of the mind,
Comes the cure from far away.
Ooooo! Ooooo!
Grow-o, Grow-o.
As you're meant to do."

Then Miss Frangipani gave
Hue Boy a bundle of herbs.
"You must have your bath
with these," she told him.
"Mind you do it every night."

For a month Hue Boy did
everything that he had been told.
Still, Hue Boy didn't grow one
little bit. He didn't grow at all,
at all.

Sometimes Hue Boy liked to go
to the harbor. Here he watched the
ships come and go, and he could
forget about his size.
    One day a beautiful big ship came in.
    Man, that looks good! thought Hue Boy.
It's the biggest ship I ever saw!

Then he saw a very tall man
among the passengers. The tall
man walked straight toward him.
"Hello, Hue Boy," he said.
"Papa!" cried Hue Boy.

His father took Hue Boy's
hand and they walked away from
the harbor and into the village.

They walked past Miss Frangipani.
They walked past Doctor Gamas and the wisest
man in the village.
They walked past Miss Harper and Carlos.
And they walked past Hue Boy's friends from school.
Then they met Gran and Mama.

And Hue Boy walked tall, with his head held high.
He was the happiest boy in the village.

And he didn't feel small at all, at all.